MELODY FOR A BROKEN MIND

By

Ken Davies

Table of Contents

Dedication

This collection of words and thoughts are dedicated to all those 'souls' lost at sea; both physically and metaphorically.

Acknowledgement

I would like to thank my resourceful and supportive wife and give special thanks to the people of Malta whose history I have been deeply touched by. My gratitude to the Editors of Amazon Publishing Agency of course, who make sure all the 'i's are dotted; and the line is crossed. And last but not least, thanks to the British Royal Navy who, although I may not have realised or fully appreciated at the time, gave me the privilege to travel, learn a little, ponder on life; and the experiences to build this story around.

Foreword

It's not always straightforward how and why we find ourselves in the situation we are in. There can be a myriad of interrelated reasons and chance happenings that whisk us along the road of our lifetime. At various points, we come across characters who have arrived at the same place as we have; but have sometimes travelled very different journeys. They all have their own story, but sadly; most of them will never be told. This book gives some glimpses into the lives of some real people; and although their names have been changed, many of the situations that are described are based on real events...

About the Author

When the author left school at sixteen, he joined the engineering branch of the British Royal Navy, while the 1970's passed by. But in this story, he draws on some of his experiences 'on board' as well as from the places his ships visited.

He married, too, during the seventies and had three children. Feeling tired of being sea-sick, he swapped the 'life on the ocean waves' for a land-based marine engineering job for a while.

For the last forty years or so, he and his wife have lived in a small seaside town in the Southwest of England, both working as teachers. His children and grandchildren are living nearby.

Having recently retired, he has been able to enjoy a little more time writing as well as walking and cycling and enjoying all that the lovely outdoors offers.

One Maltese night in 1975

Her story never crossed his mind. In the company of other drunken sailors, it just seemed ridiculous and amusing that someone of her age would be in the bar wanting to get to know them. They all knew her as 'Sweet Sixteen.' She was in her fifties; and dressed like the younger women that also frequented the bars of 'Strait Street'. It may have been somewhat out of the ordinary; but it was just another bizarre sight to be added to the others he had encountered on his voyage of enlightenment that the navy had provided him with, over the last two years.

She was fascinating, not just for her unconventional behaviour but much more by the way she outshone the pathetic figure of fun she appeared to young guys - enjoying some time away from their ship. It was easy to see her as a tragic joke; and the ethos of the 'mess deck' village didn't allow for many charitable thoughts for women and the range of circumstances they may find themselves in. Not that the prevalent concerns and behaviour of the civilian society, beyond their peculiar ironclad village, were generally much better in the 1970's: but the all male environment on board ships had the tendency to act as an 'amplifier' - reinforcing some of its 'worst attitudes'.

How could they know how she found herself there; why would it cross their minds?

Everything was a joke when you were 'ashore' and wrapped in the alcoholic insulation that kept 'real life' - with all its difficult demands; and sadly, it's simple, worthy rewards; distant and blurred.

1

"Get it down ya Tomo." Desy's command broke through his observation of her and brought his thoughts back to his fellow dissolute 'villagers'. They had put another pint in front of him. He took a gulp before realising it had more spirits in than beer. It was his eighteenth birthday and this was how he was expected to celebrate. He had already had several drinks bought for him; and their effects were taking their toll on his ability to appreciate the evening. His fellow celebrators were definitely enjoying themselves much more than he was. He knew he wouldn't last the night at the pace they were setting for him and he told them he needed some fresh air. He didn't care anymore that he would be thought of as a 'lightweight;' their gift of poison had damaged him enough. And making his unsteady way outside, the cool twilight air did its best to make him feel less bad.

After ten minutes walking aimlessly around the old town he came across a large flat piece of stone that must once have been intended for a grand building, now lost in antiquity. It invited him to sit down, gaze at the stars; and review things. Where was his life going? If this was what it was all about, it was very disappointing.

Back on board ship, he'd seen some of the old 'three badge men' who had spent the best years of their lives 'seeing the world;' but only from the inside of every bar a ship could take you to. There had to be more to it than that; there had to be more to look forward to than just the next opportunity to get too wrecked to know or care where you were!

Who had he become? How had it happened? The cool hard resilience of the stone beneath him, contrasted with his own fragility; seeming almost to insist that he question his own reality. He looked out and beyond, on what was truly visible; and did what many had done before, reflected on the imponderable: Why?

All the while, the deleterious drink; and the night time company of the unknowable stars above, conspired to induce an uncertain sense of presence, and to confuse even, when was he?

He didn't know how long he'd been sitting there - regretting some of the career choices he'd made; when it occurred to him that he must have deserted his 'birthday party' for too long. He wasn't sure where he was: or the way back to the Strait Street drinking establishments, known to every old sailor as 'the Gut'; but he felt sure he could just follow his nose.

It wasn't long before the famous cobbled narrow street, no wider than an alleyway, came into sight. The place he'd left his party goers in, was now still very much open, but there was no sign of them inside. He decided he had to ask at the bar how long ago they had left; thinking it would cut down on the time checking out every other bar on the strip looking for them.

On his way to the bar he took in the blend of cultures that made up the atmospheric fabric of the inside of the building, that he hadn't noticed before. The room had seen a lot of 'matlows' over the years, and many had left various mementos on the walls - which vied for prominence among the local photos and artwork. The randomness of their chronology and nationality; together with the incongruously modern music blaring from a jukebox that had also seen some of those better days, only added to its enchantment.

Passing some of the locals that were happily dancing to "The air that I breathe" by the Hollies; he envied them for not needing the ludicrous amount of alcohol he would need to join them, he arrived at the bar. The barman was busy drying glasses with his back to him and it gave him the chance to stare at an even more densely arranged display of 'gifts' from the world's mariners. He wondered, who were

3

these fellow travellers? And why, they had felt the compulsion to provide their own unique contribution, to the inexplicable assortment of token identities, that surrounded the optics?

At the very top of the collection were two framed photographs of aircraft.

The first one he recognised as a German Stuka dive bomber from World War Two - he'd seen many images of them from comics he'd read as a kid and in war films. The second one he couldn't identify but guessed by its appearance that it would be from the same era. When the barman eventually noticed him, he asked him about his friends. There hadn't been that many British sailors in the bar that night, so the barman knew who he meant and told Tomo they had left over an hour ago. He had no chance of reuniting with them now; and after a while thinking about what he should do next; he asked the barman if he could have a glass of water and added: "What's the plane on the right of the Stuka?" Walking away to get his drink he gave Tomo an answer that only increased his puzzlement.

"It's an Italian Savoia - Marchetti S.M.79." He called out to him, almost spitting out the words. On the barman's return he continued. "You're going to ask me why now aren't you?" "Well yer, I was kinda wondering." Tomo muttered sheepishly. "They are there because I forget many things these days; but I don't want to forget those devils." Many, many of them bombed this island to hell during the war: and many good people suffered and died here because of them." His Maltese accent seemed stronger now as he appeared more upset." "I was only a kid at the time but it has left its mark on all of us who were here then."

" We were bombed around the clock day after day, week after week, month after month." "So, so much destruction…." He stopped

4

looking at Tomo and lowered his eyes to the drink-worn timber of the bar counter. There was an awkward silence before Tomo feebly replied "I'm sorry I asked, I didn't mean to touch on such a... a raw nerve." The silence between them continued again; both of them lost for what to say. Eventually the barman recovered some of his earlier 'collected self' and came back with "Well at least you know now why us older ones are all a bit crazy."

One of the locals of a similar age to the barman, had arrived at the bar and heard some of what was being spoken about. He stared seemingly through and beyond Tomo and almost wistfully muttered "Thirty five years ago it started..." "You guys just see this island as just another place to come and play." "You know nothing of what happened to us here in nineteen forty." "You should pray you never do know what it is like." Tomo had to admit that he had no idea that the war had come to them there in such a terrible way. He knew that back in Lancashire, his own father's family had been 'bombed out' of their home in a road that now no longer existed, some time in the early forties; but he hadn't really given it much thought. He vaguely remembered that his auntie had talked about being down in an air raid shelter when she was a teenager (and when his dad would have been about nine or ten).

After the 'all clear' had sounded they came up to walk to their home, traumatically to find, it was now just a pile of rubble; and that the family had lost everything. ..."We had nothing but the clothes we stood up in." He remembered her saying. The phrase itself being more memorable than the real significance of that statement. But he definitely knew nothing about the bombing; and how bad it had been, where he was now.

The two older men continued recounting the horrors of their boyhoods to each other, and when they seemed to be ignoring him and went on to speculate why his generation was so ignorant to the suffering of the civilian population; he finished his water and slipped away.

As he returned to the narrow street, he felt sobered by the experience. The buildings along either side of him appeared tall and somewhat out of proportion compared to the restricted width it provided, and it reminded him of pictures he'd seen of medieval towns in England where neighbours across the street from each other were so close they could touch each other's hands. He looked up the old street admiring the characterful scars on the walls and doors that recorded the centuries of knocks and scrapes they had endured from unknown and probably, mostly unwitting assailants. 'Sweet Sixteen' was just leaving a bar a few yards further along and as he watched her, he thought she too must have been a real teenager when the hell was breaking loose there.

36 YEARS PREVIOUSLY.
(Chance).

In that warm early September of 1939, the thought of an impending war in North Africa sending its shock waves to shatter her sweet and peaceful island was unthinkable: preposterous; and yet within a year it would begin. She would never again see an Autumn so wonderful.

When she walked out of the house, the sun had been up a while. Her grandfather had built the house from huge blocks of the light grey stone, which gave the generously proportioned home its safe and sturdy appearance. Her grandfather had been able to provide so well for his family thanks to the proceeds of a somewhat dubious but lucrative trading connection he'd developed with Libya, during his 'go-getting' youth.

Making her way to the adjoining barn cum store, she collected her bicycle and wheeled it out of the courtyard and on to the dusty road beyond. The view of the harbour from her home was spectacular; but to be outside smelling the morning air, made it all the more special. The road to Valletta was rough and bumpy; but the discomfort inflicted by it was more than compensated for, by the joy of the gentle wind in her hair, a warm sun; and a shoreline that subtly brought more of itself into view as the journey continued.

When she reached the small row of shops and supply stores that sold almost everything her families' simple lifestyle required, she dismounted and propped her bicycle against a wall. Her main purpose for the trip to town was to buy some fresh vegetables, but she could not resist a quick peek in the window of the dressmakers - to see if the dress she had previously seen and admired was still there. It was;

and was just as desirable, as when she had first seen it. It wasn't a quick peek though; it was more like a long and lingering wide eyed inspection of all the delicate lines, gathers, stitches and embroidery that transformed a pretty piece of fabric into a masterpiece. One day, she promised herself; she would buy it.

She returned to her bicycle and noticed that the back tyre was flat. "Damn!" she said under her breath. "That useless road…" Placing her vegetables into the basket at the front of the bike, she was about to wheel the crippled machine to the garage (which also doubled as a bike showroom and repairers) when an 'English' voice behind her took her by surprise. "Would you like some help with that Miss?" She turned and saw a pair of enchanting eyes staring at her. And as the ensuing 'getting to know each other' conversation progressed, they seemed to have their own special way of 'filling in the gaps;' when what was being said didn't really tell the whole story.

She found him refreshingly attractive compared to other potential suitors who usually tried to bombard her with flattery. His reserved and 'unassuming' nature conveyed so much more to her than the often somewhat stilted words that he spoke quietly with her; ever could alone. She was sure she could recognise real sincerity when she saw it. But it was the way he smiled at her that really melted her heart.

It wouldn't be long before the owner of those eyes; James (Lighthouse) Eddiston, would become very familiar to her, as his ship - the cruiser H.M.S. Hartlepool, made return visits to the island. It was part of a fleet of vessels that were designed and built with a main purpose of protecting British interests; if possible by being an imposing deterrent: but if failing in that regard, by meeting any form of aggression with deadly force. Much of the crew of the ships were young though; and despite elements of their training; the navy was seen mostly as an opportunity to visit places they would otherwise have no chance of ever seeing; rather than an organisation that would have to do any real fighting.

During the years following 1918; Britain had ruled the waves mainly on reputation and presence alone. Most who thought anything; believed the losses endured only two decades earlier would never be repeated again. Nevertheless; when the skipper told them the news, there was a mix of feelings and attitudes towards his solemn announcement.

He had made the telling point that Prime Minister Chamberlain; a man that knew only too well the consequences of war, had found himself with no alternative. His ultimatum to Hitler had run its course, tragically, without its desired effect; and that Britain and Germany were now at war; again.

Now an ideology too flimsy to allow its validity and morality to be questioned or checked: and based solely on the deluded thinking of a psychotic leader, would begin to inflict its wickedness on the world; on a scale never before seen…

Those too young to remember the first world war, were more excited than worried; whereas the more worldly wise had good reason to be more apprehensive. The last time the two navies were pitted against each other, the outcome was equally costly to both sides. Many of the senior officers had been keen young midshipmen or sub lieutenants at the time of the battle of Jutland; and of those that had witnessed what went on then; only the foolhardy would relish a similar encounter.

The captain of the Hartlepool had made the navy his career and he was good at his job; but he was definitely no glory seeker. He viewed his crew's welfare as his major responsibility and knew now, it would only be a matter of time before he would have to put them all in jeopardy.

For the next ten months though, two young people from very different backgrounds had the chance for their mutual attraction and fondness for each other to develop into something much deeper. There were several visits made by Hartlepool, in between its operations throughout the Mediterranean: and they took every chance to be together; and when they couldn't; they exchanged what written communication that was possible under wartime censorship.

As a boy James Eddiston's family life had been a happy and loving one. His father was a miner at the local colliery, like his father had been before him; and although he embraced the fellowship of the dark, dirty and dangerous underground world of the workforce, he yearned to learn more about things beyond the inevitability of its insular neighbourhood. Untypically, he did not use drink to provide a temporary escape from the grime of his working existence, but instead, had found emancipation in reading and music. Learning to play the cornet and being a member of the colliery brass band had been a passion. The sweet yet sadly moving sound, seemed to reflect the essence of his life and spoke to him in a way nothing else could.

He had tactfully avoided any charge by his fellow workers of being aloof from them, and gained an acceptance as 'one of the lads' while at the same time; indulging in behaviours that were more usually associated with the ruling classes.

A tricky line to tread, but after some difficult years he had won their respect and had become their spokesman.

James' Mother had met his Father conventionally enough, at the town dance and quickly established they had a lot in common. Roy Eddiston and Molly Granger had both started their working lives at thirteen; and although Molly had left work at the local mill after the birth of James' older sister; and had loved being a Mother and wife, sometimes it was hard not wishing that there was more to life. Like Roy, she was bonded to the expectations of her respective community within the larger community. This brought a certain security but at the price of accepting that any talent for something outside of what was needed to keep family and friends well, would never have the chance to be realised.

James was born in 1919 and by the time he was fourteen he too had left school to earn his living at the pit. His father was in poor health by then and the family depended on his wage. There seemed to be an unalterable destiny at play. Both his parents wished for better things for their children: but times were still hard; the 'depression years' had bitten deep. Four years later though, his younger brother took his turn at the pithead; and encouraged by his family, James joined the Royal Navy.

Hartlepool was his first draft after training; and the ship was as new to the navy as he was; having only just finished its sea trials and 'work ups' after being commissioned the year before, in 1937.

It was modern and powerful; both in a military way; but also, of more significance to him, in the engineering sense. It had four of the latest steam turbine engines, producing over eighty thousand shaft horsepower between them, giving her a top speed of over thirty knots. She also had an impressive range of over six thousand nautical miles - at cruising speed, thanks to the new fuel oil being used that had superseded the more cumbersome and labour intensive shovelling of coal that its predecessors required.

She was heading for the 'Far East' within days of him joining her at Portsmouth. A deployment of some diplomatic significance to Japanese - British relations; but for James it was a voyage of discovery that he hadn't dared to dream of. In his letters home to his family he sent most of his pay, and he did his best to relay the sights he was experiencing; but the excitement of his descriptions were tinged with feelings of guilt. None of them had ever even left the county; he was now on the other side of the world.

Eddiston had learned the 'ropes' well; and by the time his ship was heading back on the long haul from Singapore to Cape Town, for refuelling and resupply, he was a proficient member of the boiler room team.

Under 'steady steaming' conditions - when the ship would stay at a pretty constant speed and course; the ship's steam turbines also required a constant amount of superheated steam. This was provided by the newly developed and efficient, 'Admiralty Three Drum boilers' that produced the high temperatures required for superheated steam.

Consequently, as a boiler front watch keeper he had little to do to maintain that consistency, the gas oil pumps and forced air blowers, had automated a lot of the work his predecessors had had to do. Perhaps every ten minutes or so the steam pressure would drift a fraction higher than the three hundred pounds per square inch required, and a half size burner sprayer would need to be turned off and extracted back on its rail, only to be required back on again a little later - as the pressure gauge indicated a slight drop below the magic three hundred.

This easy time was in stark contrast to periods when the ship was manoeuvring and constantly changing speed. This required various combinations of sprayers to be on and off in quick succession. In order for an additional sprayer to be in place and working properly it had to be manually pushed into the fiery furnace. Then a lever had to be turned on allowing pressurised air to provide the oxygen for the forthcoming combustion, before the lever for the gas oil was opened.

The ensuing spray of fuel and air mix would then instantly be ignited by the furnaces' existing inferno - provided by the other sprayers already operating.

When the boiler was producing too much heat and a sprayer (or more usually, a 'half sprayer') had to be retracted, the reverse procedure was needed. With practice both procedures could be done in under three seconds, but when first done by a nervous teenager, the awesome power being unleashed only inches in front of him was formidable; and each ignition could be felt as a low menacing vibration, which could also be observed through the boiler's small sight glass. But within a relatively short period of time it all became pretty second nature. The teamwork and understanding between the Petty officer in charge of the boilers and the boiler front watch keepers, had to be finely tuned. The communication between them was by hand signals, as shouting above the ambient noise of the various machinery was not really possible.

Some of the old 'sweats' told him how easy the job was now; with the new type boilers, and that not using coal meant; 'a stoker was not a stoker anymore.' There were still plenty of laborious tasks to do though; such as cleaning the 'brass work' - which served no real practical purpose other than to make it stay looking good.

Scrubbing the boiler room deck plates however, had the more useful role of preventing everyone from slipping over; particularly when the sea did its best to throw them all off balance. Then there was also the job that every lowly stoker loathed; cleaning the bilges: necessary; but unedifying to say the least.

The quieter times though, also gave him the opportunity to learn more about the ancillary machinery; and by the time he'd left South Africa on the final long leg home, he'd qualified as a stoker mechanic first class.

He crossed the equator again - this time at night and without all the ceremony that the uninitiated like him had had to go through on the journey out. When he'd first done that, on the way south many months earlier; he'd been compelled to go to the upper deck to take part in the theatrically bizarre procedure of being inducted into the domain of 'Neptunus Rexus.'' A memorable experience that recorded the crossing of the otherwise, 'unnoticeable' border between the earth's two hemispheres. And this time, after finishing the 'Middle Watch' he indulged in a less flamboyant trip to the upper deck - just to see the equatorial stars before 'turning in.' The sea air was still warm even with the breeze, but nowhere so intense that it would cause the metal handrails to burn your hands - as he had discovered the painful way, on his first time 'Crossing the Line' in the full heat of the day.

The Middle watch, from Midnight to four in the morning, was often a quieter time, though not literally, as the boiler room noise was constantly loud; but when all the routine tasks were done and the bridge was not asking for any changes of speed, there was a treat in store. This was when the team would take the opportunity to sit together and share a couple of cups of 'pot-mess'. It consisted of a mixture of the galley's leftover food from the day before. This mixture would be collected from the galley and taken to the boiler room in a large steel pot.

It amazed him to think that the boiler's original superheated steam that they had made; having now lost some of its heat energy and pressure (after powering the main engines) was not done yet. The steam may have become saturated; but it was still energetic enough to power auxiliary machinery. After that, the majority of this further depleted steam would then go on to the ship's condensers, to be turned back into boiler 'feed water,' completing the virtuous steam cycle.

Not all the steam was contained in this cycle however; and situated in the boiler room were the reciprocating pumps that could still utilise the much diminished saturated, low pressure steam. They owed their technology to a previous century when steam power was in its infancy and could not be heated to the temperatures and pressures now possible.

They seemed incongruous anachronisms as they nodded and hissed their constant steady delivery of more feed water drawn from the feed water tanks, to the ever demanding boilers. But their old fashioned design had a very fortunate unintended benefit.

A small drain constantly 'exhausted' a small amount of steam to the bilges which by chance, produced just the right amount to allow the pot to simmer nicely; and after a couple of hours; having done all its marvellous work; 'the team's' steam had this one last job to do: and it tasted all the more delicious for it.

The final member of the boiler room team was a 'killick stoker' - who was the 'evaporator' watch keeper. It was his job to 'make' the extra feed water that the system required. Again, by harnessing the heat energy of the saturated steam, this time to boil seawater; to be condensed into pure water by the cooling action of the sea. In rough weather though, this became a black art; as to keep the condensed water free of all salt - which is what the boilers demanded - required the skills of an experienced magician. When enough feed water had been 'made' to top up the feed tank though, he could join them for the feast; and the 'evaps' could be left to top up the ship's 'fresh' water tanks; as they didn't require such a high standard of purity.

Between them; the team provided the power for all of the ship's functions, as even the main electricity generators were steam powered; they also produced all of the ship's fresh water.

That was why, at the end of a sweaty watch, when they used the hot water they had 'made' for what was known as a 'bath n' dhobie', they felt more entitled to it than most.

Hartlepool arrived back in 'Pompey' at the beginning of December; and although Eddison was on duty for the first part of the Christmas leave period, he was able to see the new year of 1939 in, with his family. By mid February, and after some minor refitting; the ship was ready for its next deployment to the newly reformed Mediterranean fleet. As it set sail, wives and girlfriends on the harbour side were waving goodbye, as an icy wind off the Solent chilled all those required to be on the upper deck for 'Procedure Alpha.' Sometimes a steamy boiler-room could be a better place to be.

Eddison would not be a part of the boiler room team for long though, as he would soon be taking up his new job of 'outside machinery watch keeper'. This would entail making sure that all other machinery that was not either in the boiler or engine room was maintained and running correctly: and there was a lot of machinery between the forward spaces and the 'stern glands' and 'steering gear' in the 'tiller flats'.

The new role gave him the chance to travel the length and breadth of the ship; and even a brief moment on the upper deck; but to check everything thoroughly, every hour, was impossible. This meant that during a four hour watch, not all machinery was checked every hour; but over the four hours, everything could be checked at least once. Even so it was still exhausting, particularly when the sea was rough. He soon learned that you waited for the ship to be on the way up from the trough of a wave to lift a large steel hatch on a machinery space as, at that moment it became almost weightless. Conversely, when the ship was on the way down from a crest, it was almost too heavy to lift.

During the nearly six months of predominantly; 'sea time' - many frenetic exercises were carried out. These consisted mainly of simulated hostile engagements; where the ship would be 'closed up' for 'action stations' for hours on end. This required all the ship's steel doors and hatches to have all their retaining 'clips' in place; unlike in more relaxed times when only one or two would suffice. It made moving around the ship much more time consuming. Not good news for 'outside rounds' watch keeping.

In August; a well tuned and practised Hartlepool, was alongside in Gibraltar, for replenishment and a welcome 'run ashore.'

There was just time to climb the 'rock' and admire the unusual spectacle of the wild Barbary apes; a reminder of how close to Africa they were and not something you see everyday in mainland Europe. And of course, the 'obligatory' tour of the bars on the 'strip;' in a fleeting 'twenty four off.'

Steaming out of Gibraltar harbour; the narrowness of the strait made the coast of Morocco clear to see; clarifying the geography of the Mediterranean's gateway to and from the Atlantic. Turning to port and heading East; the ship ventured into darkening skies. Europe to the North; and Africa to the South; the sun setting into a crimson streaked Atlantic ocean to 'stern'. There were yet more joint exercises with the rest of the fleet to be carried out; but for now he had a little time before his next watch began and thought he'd take in some inviting evening sea air on the upper deck. Wandering aft, the fading light was now allowing the first stars to appear and give further perspective to understanding his place and his purpose.

He reached the guardrails and took in lung-fulls of the welcome cool breeze. Lowering his eyes he witnessed the white tumult rapidly moving away from him - a powerful disturbance to a deep blue tranquil sea, now churning white, courtesy of the tramping of eighty thousand galloping horses. The culmination of those many energy and force transfers taking place below decks; moving him and the twelve thousand tons of ship forward, at half a mile a minute.

Soon it would be his turn again to play his part in creating and keeping control of all that awesome power.

The next port of call though, would be his, and the ship's; first visit to Malta. He had no more expectancy about it, than there had been with any of the other places visited. He felt privileged to have seen so much already in his young life - and often thought about what life could have been like if he had stayed in his hometown. The range and boundaries of experiences he'd been so lucky to have had thus far though, were about to be vastly expanded: and the time frame in which it would be lived, so compressed; it would test the endurance of everything he consisted of. There was not an inkling of what emotional joy he would find there - in the arms of someone so unimaginable - nor the depth of despair that was to await him.

Hartlepool entered the peaceful waters of Malta's Grand Harbour twenty days after war was declared between Britain and Germany;

and the skipper had given them that sobering news. But the only real hostilities involving the Royal Navy were taking place in the North Atlantic: and they felt a long way away. The 'phoney war' was being played out: and all the visits to the Island the ship made, through the Autumn of 1939; until the end of Spring of 1940, were equally peaceful, with enemy aggression only simulated with yet more exercises, when returning to sea.

This was their time. And it was so wonderful for both of them. During one of their long walks together she had found out that his workmates (or 'oppos;' as he referred to them), called him 'Lighthouse' - because his surname was very similar to the name of a lighthouse that was built on a small outcrop of rocks, off the southwest coast of England. And every ship's crew member had a nickname of some sort. She loved his 'nickname' and thought it suited him. And whenever he was back on his ship and there was a moon that shone its silver path of light across the sea, from the horizon to her harbour, it was his comforting signal to her. Her lighthouse…

TRIBULATION.

By early June, though, his ship sailed again; and this time, its voyage was very different. It was in very real action within days. For her, too, the foul taste of war was in the air as the first Italian bombs began falling on Malta.

As the summer progressed, his ship never made it back to Grand Harbour; but daily she looked out to its waters, seeing only the distressing sight of other battle damaged ships occasionally coming in for repairs. Most of them were en-route to - or from Alexandria, endeavouring to keep The Eighth Army supplied, as it fought the advancing Italian forces, threatening to take Egypt from the British. At the same time, the bombing on Malta, that had been sporadic at first, was intensifying. Life was anything but normal now.

Two days after the Italians declared war, Hartlepool was shelling Italian positions near Tobruk, when it came under fire from Italian ships. Real shells causing real harm. It sustained minor damage and casualties before its six - inch guns sank one of its attackers and the remainder broke away.

In July, Italian torpedo bombers attacked Hartlepool while it was heading out from Alexandria; but the damage was also relatively light and it was still able to function - after carrying out running repairs. Despite this official description of 'minor damage and casualties;' Eddiston had been shocked when he first saw what battle damage really looked like, both to the soft flesh of men; and to the previously unquestioned integrity of steel plate rendered contorted and ruptured.

It was a rapid transition from relative 'sprog' to experienced hand on board a warship at war; and by September he was already feeling more hardened and resolved to his lot. There had always been a good sense of camaraderie on board, but since the enemy action had started, that shared experience had bonded everyone much tighter.

In the quieter moments though, he had time to think about all the wonderful days he had shared with her; and he longed to be walking; laughing; and holding her again. The times they had shared seemed all the more special now.

At the end of September He was unexpectedly back. Hartlepool had been escorting a convoy from Gibraltar; and had done its best to fend off yet more attacks, but some had succeeded in inflicting more destruction, particularly on one of the hapless 'merchantmen' supply ships. A silent killer from beneath the waves, not some mythical sea monster, but something only too real; and much more sinister. Something so deadly effective, only intelligent minds and human ingenuity could devise; the 'u boat' torpedo.

Encased within its innocuous looking appearance, a torpedo had the ability to send a ship full of human lives, to the bottom of the sea in a few panic stricken minutes.

He had seen at first hand, the desperate look on the faces of the survivors dragged on board from an unforgiving sea of black. The stench of fuel oil that covered everyone and everything, stung his eyes; and conspired with the ship's wallowing motion to assault his stressed brain's vomit centre. He'd thrown up so much that there was only bile left to spit out.

All of them did their best for the sunken ship's crew; but the cruiser's sick bay had neither enough medical equipment or personnel to meet the needs of the dying. The upper deck was strewn with a damnation of barely recognisable humanity.

Hartlepool and two other ships made all available speed to Malta, while the rest of the convoy continued on to Alexandria. There was little time, or ability to sleep on the journey - that in different circumstances would have been so welcome. Once alongside, frantic evacuation of surviving wounded, was assisted by waiting civilian and military personnel and a rapid programme of repair and replenishment was begun. The skipper gave six hours of leave to all those who could be spared; but it was a numb, haggard young man that made his way down the gangway, and onto a dry land that felt like it was heaving.

The contrast to how, only a few months ago, he'd felt such a spring in his step and a lightness in his heart, went unnoticed by a distracted world.

As her house came into view, he could immediately see it too was suffering from the ravages of a war from the skies. Several of its windows were now covered with what looked like the parts of packing crates and other odd shaped pieces of wood. Coming closer, he could also see cracks that jagged their way down the side of one of its walls: but it still stood - much as it had always had - an epitaph to the pride and passion of her grandfather. Despite the random pocked infliction of Italian bomb craters on the innocent hillside around, it too defied all attempts to do much to reduce its charm. The afternoon sun did its best to light the building's attractive and defiantly powerful form - and it remained - in keeping with the surroundings that embraced it: still, both the better for each other's company.

She was soft, beautiful and full of comfort. The sight of her drained his anger at the world and emptied his head of the hellish images that had stained his time awake; and haunted his nights. She was alone in her house - her father, had gone to Valletta where the bomb damage had been much more severe; and he was needed to help clear rubble from the many bomb - damaged homes.

The sight of Edditson shocked her; but she tried not to show it, and ran to him. They held each other, with so few words being spoken but with so much being told. The desperation of feelings, the sense of such little time to be together, led him to go further with his passion than he'd allowed himself to before - she too, could not help herself.

They picked themselves up from the cool flagstones of the sitting room and composed themselves for a walk out into the hillside sunshine. They recalled a beautiful Spring, swimming at Rinella bay, and listening to Irving Berlin sing 'How deep is the Ocean' on her wind - up phonograph, as they wandered, trying to delude themselves that the next few hours were an eternity. The words to that song; their song; so sweetly set to music, but so bitterly poignant.

He knew he had to leave her and return to his ship; but he had to fight every instinct that pleaded with him to desert his responsibilities to his comrades and his country: and stay in the warmth and gentleness of her love.

It was a lonely, empty walk back to the Hartlepool. And to what had once seemed a sight of prestige and pride - a marvel of modern marine engineering; now transfigured into a vision of inescapable horror.

She watched his ship leave her harbour, her island, her life, and cursed the foolishness of mankind for its self-destructiveness....

Edditson regained consciousness in Alexandria's military hospital. He had no recollection of hearing the explosion in the forward compartment of the cruiser - while he was on his 'outside rounds'; nor the secondary explosion and fireball caused by the

23

leaking fuel from the forward tanks, that blew him off his feet and burnt him down his left side. That October, very few of the twenty seven-dead; and thirty-five injured crew had known anything about the torpedo, launched from the Savoia - Marchetti aircraft. For many of them, life ended instantly; but for the unfortunate; it took until the early hours of the following morning before they found their peace. All were buried at sea as the crippled ship, and her surviving crew found their individual ways of 'carrying on': all the time knowing that annihilation from the air, the surface of the sea; or especially from below it, could so easily be their fate too.

It was less than a hundred nautical miles back to Alexandria - but the cruiser was so badly hit that it had to be towed there - stern first - by an accompanying cruiser, losing a substantial section of her bow on the way.. and at towing speed, it seemed to take an age.

LONDON 1945.
A wartime between.

Third officer Kitty Simmons had joined the Royal Navy as a 'Wren,' wanting to 'do her bit' - soon after hearing Neville Chamberlain's radio broadcast, solemnly telling the country that Britain was now at war with Germany (in that same Autumn of '39). She hadn't really thought exactly what job she would do, but had definitely not thought she would be spending much of her time over the last six years, writing to hapless families informing them of their loss.

"Sir, this is the eighth letter we've received from this Maltese lady." She is trying to find out about a crew member on the cruiser Hartlepool." "At the time of her first letter, the cruiser had been attacked by Italian torpedo bombers, and there had been several crew killed, but the name of the sailor she is asking about was not on that list. "Since then, though sir, I've been sent the list of the wounded... and he appears to be on it."

Lieutenant Commander Brian Collins lifted his gaze from the papers that he was reading - and looked at her over his spectacles. "What were the extent of his injuries"? His voice matching the tired indifference showing in his eyes, acquired from dealing with more tragic stories than he cared to dwell on.

"He had second degree burns and severe concussion leading to amnesia, sir." "Well, what are you bothering me about her letters for?" "He'll never remember her anyway." "I take it they weren't" married?" "No sir, they weren't; but previously she claimed to be carrying his child." He looked at her in silence; but his expression told her that he'd heard that hard luck story a thousand times, and; was she really that naive? "It's just that in her latest letter she has sent a photo of herself with him; and a separate one of the child; and I just thought that it might help to jog his memory."

"Look; - don't you think he's been through enough already; the last thing he needs is some tart chasing him for money." "But she's not asking for anything like that sir, she just wants to know if he's alive or dead." Indignation now leaking into her voice. "They never do ask for money to start with; but as soon as you confirm anything, you'll never hear the last of it from her." " You know the policy, - just write to her expressing your deepest sympathy etc. - etc.- but unfortunately, you can find no record of him; okay ..." He knew he sounded callous, but he was sure from some bitter experience that it would be better for all concerned. "Yes, sir."

As she left his office she thought about how she could possibly craft a letter that would not dash all hope for a young woman who seemed not so dissimilar from herself.

Someone who had just had the misfortune of falling for the right person at a very wrong time. It would need some thought to do that, while still relaying the message her superior officer had just demanded of her. When she got back to her desk, the priority pile of paperwork that needed to be dealt with, meant she had to give it her attention first; and she placed the young women's letters in her desk drawer.

A Grand Harbour 1975

Tomo decided he'd skip a few bars as there would be more chance of finding his party; but after checking out a few more of them, he decided to just try one more. It was much quieter than the places he had visited, with only a few locals in. He bought himself a coffee and sat away from anyone, thinking how he could justify 'shooting through' on his own party, but all of his excuses seemed pretty lame. The seat was comfortable though, too comfortable, and despite the coffee; he fell asleep….

No! Surely not, five minutes to midnight? How could he have not kept an eye on the time. He knew the last dghajsa would be leaving at that Cinderella hour. Getting to his feet, he rushed out the door and ran as fast as he could down Strait Street. By the time custom house steps came into sight, his lungs felt like they were bursting, and he was fighting the urge to spew. He kept running until he could just make out the shape of the little boat chugging its way out into the harbour from the mooring - its wake producing perfect silvery white ripples, spreading their way across the inky waters.

At the top of the old white steps that lead down to the harbour's edge, he stopped to catch his breath and ponder his predicament.

That little boat was how he was going to get back to his ship - now, what was he going to do? There was no sign of any taxis and definitely no buses running at that time of night. He soon realised his only option was to walk right around Grand harbour. He had to be back 'on board ship' before eight in the morning when his next watch began, or he would be in the 'proverbial.'

If he kept the harbour to his left, he knew it must eventually lead him to the old jetty at Fort Ricasoli - at the mouth of the harbour, where his ship was 'tied up' alongside - but how big was the harbour? It took the dghajsas about twenty minutes by water, but that was a much shorter route - how long would it take to walk the long way round? He'd never really thought about it before - although he'd been to the antiquated harbour for 'a run ashore' - a few times before on his previous ship H.M.S. Whitby. Sadly, that was now being broken up for scrap metal, back in Portsmouth; a sombre end to a fine little ship.

At first, there were still the lights of Valletta to see his way by - but soon, the street lights petered out, and the buildings along the harbour's edge became more dilapidated. It was clear that no one had lived in them for some time. After walking for another couple of miles, past more of what looked like broken-down cafes, bars and homes - that tumbled down to the melancholy waterside, he was struck by the contrast they made to the vibrancy of the capital he had left behind - with all its neon illumination and recorded music.

He stood there, listening to the quiet of the small hours of the morning: soaking up the scene before him. Between the heaps of dereliction, there were still glimpses of that ancient harbour which had provided the means for the comings and goings of so many different peoples over the centuries.

He was very much alone now, with only the gentle waves breaking on the rocky shore, whispering their timeless murmurs to interrupt the silence. A little further on, the moonlight picked out a stone archway that caught his eye. As he got closer, he saw it was an ornate doorway into what must have been once - a fine house. Inside, some remnants of furniture and the possessions of former occupants could just be made out - as the moon did its best to scatter its pastel light onto them.

Curiosity got the better of him, and he diverted from the path to take a closer look. Rubble and fragments of tiles from a long gone roof, along with some of the upstairs walls, covered the floor. Parts of smashed tables, crushed cabinets, upturned chairs and unrecognisable fabrics were all jumbled among the debris.

At the far end of the destruction, a battered flight of stairs were still almost intact, although a large splintered roof beam and torn pieces of floor board, along with yet more rubble, made access difficult. He knew he should really leave and make sure he had enough time to get back to his ship but he felt compelled to see what was up those stairs.

He quickly cleared most of the rubble out of the way along with the easy to move boards, but some were jammed under the heavy beam, so he clambered over them - clearing other debris as he began climbing the remaining stairs. He was nearly at the top when - without warning, there was a blinding flash of jagged light followed instantly by darkness. Still, silent, darkness.

Gradually sound and light returned. He could see again, but what sights.

The landing was in wonderful condition, not at all like the mess that was downstairs. It was also much more spacious than he had imagined it would be, with panelling on the walls that looked as if they might have been reclaimed from shipwrecks long ago. The Floor, too, was of beautiful polished wood, covered with huge patterned rugs with several large doors leading from it to other rooms. The high ceiling was not just intact but decorated with wonderfully ornate plaster-work with iron gas lights hanging from it. He stared for some time, enjoying the splendour, when one of the substantial doors opened.

A young woman walked out onto the landing in front of him. The first thing he noticed - apart from how pretty she looked - with her dark eyes and raven hair - was that she was dressed in quite an old-fashioned way.

She also looked as surprised to see him as he was to see her. They both stood still, just staring at each other for some time before he gathered his senses enough to say, "Please excuse me - I didn't think anyone lived here." " I hope I didn't frighten you." After quite another long pause, the girl replied in quite a strong accent. "Who the hell are you?"

He told her his name and that he was just on his way back to his ship. "What ship? What is the name of your ship?" "H.M.S. Norfolk" - he quickly responded. "I have never heard of this ship: and from my window, I see all the ships that come into the harbour." "Now tell me the truth!" "I am telling you the truth." He insisted. "It's a GMD - you know a county class destroyer, same as Devonshire, Antrim, Glamorgan and the others - you must have seen plenty of them come and go; they've been coming here since the sixties." "No!" "I Haven't;" she complained. "Everything you are telling me doesn't sound true - and what do you mean by the sixties?" Her voice now full of disdain. "And why are you dressed so strangely?"

He looked down at his jeans, t-shirt and plimsolls, and they seemed to him the only normal thing about the situation, while the jacket and skirt she was wearing looked quite dowdy, but he thought it would be a bit rude to say so, considering he was evidently in her house. Instead, he thought it would be best to leave before she got any more aggravated with him."

I'm afraid I usually dress like this when I'm in 'civies,' if I had known how things would turn out, I would have made more of an effort; and yes, I did mean the nineteen sixties you know the Beatles, mini skirts, man on the moon and all that...." His attempt at explanation tailed off as he could see from the even more perplexed look on her face, that he was probably just making things worse for himself.

He tried to make his apologies again, when she interjected. Her tone sounding slightly less harsh and her accent much more charming. "Who are you really?" "I told you, I'm Jack Thompson, my friends call me 'Tomo' - I'm a 'stoker' on the Norfolk." "We only arrived here yesterday, well, the day before yesterday now."

"I'm really sorry for coming into your home, but as I said, It looked derelict from outside and I was just.." "Derelict?" she interrupted with quizzical indignation. "Well, you know, from the outside it looks like a bomb's hit the place." As the words left his mouth, he instantly realised that they must have sounded insulting and he tried to correct himself; when she came back with: "Well, that bloody rat Mussellini has been sending his bombers to try to kill us all since June; but so far we've been lucky here, any bomb damage is mainly to the airfields and in the centre of Valletta." "I don't know what you think you saw outside."

Her words stunned him. He remembered the conversation with the barman and his old pal about when the bombing started in Malta. The 10th of June 1940 was when the Italians had declared war, and that it was the start of more than three years of continual air raids that destroyed so much of the island's buildings.

His mouth was dry as he looked into her eyes, and he could hardly speak. "What ... year are we in?" he asked tentatively. "I know it's a stupid thing to say but please answer my question." "I'm the one who should be asking the questions." she retorted; but after a tense pause,

31

she began; " Well I don't know about you strange man, but its 1940 here."

A thousand thoughts were racing around his head. The 'Norfolk' had only left Italy a couple of weeks ago, where he and his mates had had a great 'run ashore' in Venice, and it was all very congenial - now it seemed quite likely that he could be bombed by some very unfriendly Italians. What was going on? Nothing made sense. He'd joined the Norfolk a few months ago in January, but that was definitely 1975, not 1940!

His state of mind and the drawn look on his face must have spooked her, for the next thing he heard was her shouting, "Missier!" He had no idea what it meant, but he soon found out; as behind him, he could hear the sound of someone, or something heavy coming up the stairs.

As he turned to see what it was, a large man was just ascending the last few stairs. Those same stairs that he had climbed, covered in all that wreckage. Now they were in a similar pristine condition to the rest of the landing. The man saw him and rapidly increased his pace towards him; he had a pick axe handle in his right hand and a look of fury in his eyes.

The girl spoke quickly to the man, again in Maltese, and he slowed his approach. "This is my father; I've told him not to kill you:... yet." He couldn't be sure from the way she spoke or the look on her face if she was serious, but he was feeling a little relieved that he wasn't in immediate danger of being killed by a 1940's pick axe handle. She continued speaking to her father in Maltese, and he assumed she was relaying to him his explanation of why he was in their house, which he worried wouldn't sound very convincing. Her father spoke back to her, and after they'd been in conversation for some time, the girl explained that her father thought that he may be an Italian or German spy and wanted to hand him over to the authorities.

He immediately protested his innocence. "I'm British; what can I do to prove it to you?" He went to get his wallet from his pocket and her father swiftly raised the wooden handle as if to strike him. "I'm just going to show you my ID card - it's in my pocket." In a menacing reply; and in an even stronger accent than the girl's, her father then commanded that he should "Do it slowly."

He hadn't realised that her father spoke English, but he was glad that he did and he told him so. "Of course I speak English, everybody on the island speaks English; we've been governed by the British since 1813, you idiot." "Okay, I'm sorry I wasn't sure."

He showed his ID, but this did not impress them. "That's not a standard issue card." Her father snapped. He was right - he'd not thought it through - 1940's ID cards, if they existed at all, probably looked very different from his 1970's photo one. Even if it was similar, it now occurred to him that a spy would, at the very least, be issued with fake ID. His hopes of convincing them of his true identity were failing fast.

They took his wallet from him and went through its contents. His latest pay packet was in there, together with what was left of his pay. His first thought was to say, 'take the money - but just let me get back to my ship.' Then he thought better of it as it would probably be seen as a bribe and, make him seem more guilty. Her father looked at the pay packet and then at him "This is a navy pay packet." " Did you steal it?" "No" - he replied indignantly, "It's my pay packet, my wallet and I am who I say I am." Her father looked at the date on the pay packet and read out loud, "1975" It was her father's turn to be confused - why that date? If it was a forgery, both the Italians and Germans knew what year it was; why wouldn't they have put the correct year, 1940, on the packet?

He could tell that her father was beginning to feel less hostile towards him. There was also a letter from his girlfriend back in England in the wallet, and its postmark also read 1975. Her father may have become more friendlier, but he was very much more confused. He suggested all three of them should go downstairs and sit at the table. What table? Tomo thought the last time he saw downstairs - what remained of it was in pieces and covered in rubble; but as he came downstairs the sight of the room startled him. Like the landing upstairs, there was beautiful panelling on the walls on which several paintings of seascapes and old sailing ships were hanging. There were windows on three sides that were letting large streaks of light shine in on the room. Tomo had seen so many inexplicable things, that the fact that it was daylight outside, when his wrist watch said two forty-five in the morning - didn't seem worth wondering more about.

Along the rear of the room, three windows looked out onto the harbour. From them, he could see a variety of fishing boats were pulled up onto the shoreline, and a scattering of fishermen were mending nets and carrying out other minor repairs and maintenance tasks. Anchored out in the perfect azure of the harbour, there was what appeared to be an old and somewhat dilapidated looking small ship.

At its stern, he could just make out a white ensign gently fluttering in a light breeze.

The girl was the first to sit down at the substantial farmhouse table occupying the centre of the room. Tomo was told, rather than invited, to sit opposite. The girl's father then sat at the head of the table, closest to the hallway and the way out. Once the three of them were seated, the girl was the first to speak. "My name is 'Marija.' That's Mary in English." She informed him; "And my father is Awgustu. "Nice to meet you." he said; instantly feeling the inappropriateness of his remark. "I'll happily go with you to the authorities, " he added; " if we can somehow clear-up what the heck is going on." "I'm sure we all will…." Before he could finish his sentence the growing sound of aircraft engines were drowning out his words....

He awoke with dust in his mouth and a slow throbbing pain in his head. Touching the part of his head that hurt the most, he was shocked to feel the wetness. He took his hand away - to look at the dark liquid that now covered his hand, but in the half light that the moon was providing, he couldn't make out its colour - but it was pretty obvious what it was. He looked up and could see the stairs next to him. They were much as he'd first seen them - covered in the years of decay that had collapsed from above, but part of the top section was missing along with a section of banisters.

I must have fallen from them, he told himself. That will teach me to go exploring in the middle of the bloody night. Picking himself up, he cursed his foolishness and scrambled his way out of the building. It wasn't just his head that hurt now, he was hobbling on a painful ankle, and the left side of his ribs ached with certain movements. As he got to the doorway that led outside; he again noticed how the moonlight caught the ornate detail on its frame. He stood there for a minute admiring its form and proportion; and gave himself some time to gather his senses before resuming his quest to get back to H.M.S Norfolk.

He continued as before, finding the best path that kept the harbour to his left. Soon he had passed the last few remains of old buildings, and he was in more open country - rugged and wild - it seemed that not much had changed here for a very long time. Perhaps the last people to live there were from some ancient civilisation, or even cavemen, he thought to himself. The arcane scenery continued for another mile or so, and then as he got to the top of the rise in the path, he could see further in the direction he was heading for. In the distance, he could just make out some tiny lights, partially illuminating an otherwise dark object. It was definitely man-made as it did not blend in with the paleness of the rocky shoreline leading to it and would be about the right shape and proportion of Norfolk. The sight of it gave a renewed energy to his pace.

As he got to the gangway, he looked at his watch. It read 0420. That's great, he thought; I've just got time for a couple of hours sleep before 'turning to.' At the top of the gangway he met his mate 'Topsy Turner,' who was duty watch on deck. After exchanging some not so pleasant 'pleasantries' and some general teasing - along the lines of 'what the heck happened to you?' - he made his way to the 'heads' to clean himself up before heading down to his mess-deck. Its claustrophobic steel darkness and familiar background whine of nearby machinery, now oddly reassuring.

The next morning the cut on his head was healing and was mainly obscured by his slightly longer than 'regulation' hair; but it still throbbed as he travelled around the ship checking on the various machinery on his 'outside' rounds. As did his ribs when negotiating hatches and the many sets of ladders. When he came to the upper deck to check on the gas turbine 'genny,' he could see Valletta far in the distance; and he thought he could just make out the part of the harbour-side where the tumbled-down houses were - and where he must have had his accident. The image of the house looking so pristine - and the people seemed all so vivid though.

He'd been knocked unconscious once before when he was a kid in the 'cubs' - he'd run into one of the bigger boys and then fell backwards, hitting the back of his head on the floor.

Apparently, he was taken home by the cub master, still unconscious, before 'coming to' some minutes later. No hospital or doctor was involved - but all he could recall of the incident was waking up to see lots of familiar but concerned faces staring down at him. He definitely couldn't remember having any dreams while he was out.

LONDON 1980. A duty given, the task ahead.

"Welcome, ladies and gentlemen: as I know you are all well aware; today - is Kitty's last day with us after forty one years of dedicated service...."

Her boss' speech extolling the great work she had done, over all those years - was quite 'cringy' for her to have to sit through. She had attended many such tributes to previous colleagues, but it was different when it was you receiving all that glowing praise. The speech seemed to go on forever as the rest of the audience occasionally responded more with polite laughter; rather than any true amusement to the supposed 'funny bits.' When it finally came to an end though, the punchline was the presentation of her old desk. It was the same desk that she'd been given to work at - on her first day in the office. It was old then; and had apparently been donated by a 'titled lady' who wanted to make a contribution to the newly reformed 'Women's Royal Naval Service' that was being hastily resourced. Kitty had loved it immediately.

The desk was an Edwardian ladies' writing desk, with two shallow main drawers underneath - that together, ran along its full length, and each extended its full width. Two sets of three smaller drawers were located in the middle of the top of the desk, set back to still allow plenty of space for writing. 'Outboard' of each of these were two cabinets of the same height and with their own doors. Its legs, when viewed from the side, were of an inverted heart shape for their top half, with their lower half tastefully fluted and splayed, resting on brass clawed feet. The natural pattern and colouration of the wood grain encapsulated all the autumn colour of a horse-chestnut 'conker.'

She had managed to stay in possession of it through several office moves and refurbishments, as well as the re-organisations that had called for 'modern' furniture, and she'd had had to fight for its continued existence many times. But the two of them had stayed together while colleagues and loved ones passed - and the world changed. Now they would be leaving together.

When it was delivered to her home, she had it take pride of place in the room she rather grandly referred to as the 'library.' In reality, it was quite a small room that also doubled as the sitting room. One of its walls had been recently fitted with shelves and was now filled with an eclectic selection of reading material that had previously been occupying various odd places around the house. The good thing about retirement - was having the opportunity to reorganise and re-invent the house she would be spending a lot more time in.

Once she had hoped that the house would be shared by the man she loved, but that wasn't to be: and it had taken the healing power of many busy years of distraction to come to terms with that devastating reality.

Her desk looked right there, and as she stood there admiring how it enhanced the look of the room, she also thought about what needed to occupy all the various drawers and compartments that gave it that rare combination of beauty and utility. But first, it needed; and deserved some renovation - and today she would put to the test - all the things she'd learned on the furniture restoration course she had just completed at evening classes. It was time to give it the new life she imagined for it.

Most of its carcass was in remarkably good condition despite the many years of less than careful treatment it had endured following its enrolment into military service - and its rejuvenation was relatively straightforward. The right-hand cabinet was a different matter though. For some time, its door had become quite difficult to open and close, and she had 'made do' with using the rest of the desk's other ample storage spaces.

In fact, it had been so long since she had put anything in it - that she wasn't really sure what was still in there; but she had reassured herself that if it had been anything important, she would have transferred it to the working cabinet on the left side, long ago.

Trying to open it now by using its small ornately cast handle, was proving to be a real test for her newly acquired skills. She felt if she pulled it too hard, it was so delicate it might break; so she employed the widest bladed screwdriver she possessed to help lever it open. After prising the door at several positions along its edge, whilst simultaneously pulling at its fragile handle, it eventually eased open. She felt so pleased with her success that she didn't take much notice of what was in it at first; instead, checking what damage the screwdriver may have caused to the door and its surround. Thankfully it was minimal, and she felt confident she could repair what minor indentations that were there, quite easily.

Removing the contents of the cabinet later, she came across some old photos of her and some of her previous colleagues. How time had changed her; and no doubt, them; as most of them, she had not seen in a long time. There were also some copies of old 'standing orders' and various other not very useful officious documentation; that she would happily tear up. At the bottom of the pile of paperwork though, were eight envelopes held together with one of her old hair ribbons.

Immediately she saw them; it took her back to that time in the latter stages of the war when she had hurriedly squirrelled them away, fully intending to answer them. The detail of the letters escaped her, but she remembered that they had seemed important at the time and was shocked they had been overlooked for so long. Reading them again upset her all the more. She had not responded to them - and it shamed her. Of course she had been busy; of course there was a war on: but... It was becoming clear now what happened.

It must have been only a few days after putting the letters there that she had gotten the news about her father. He was a fifty-two year old police sergeant who had worked for the force for over thirty years. He had experienced many incidents during that time, but the years of the blitz and the V1 'doodle bugs' had been the toughest.

Attending the bomb sites immediately after they had happened was not for the faint-hearted; and some of the gruesome things that he had dealt with had taken their toll on him. Kitty couldn't help but notice how he'd become more distant and serious. The smiles and hugs were still there, but they felt very different. He never spoke to her about his work, but she knew it would not be unusual for him to be the first 'on the scene' having to try and rescue people of all ages that were injured; dying or dead from the wreckage of buildings and often, their own homes.

But like so many of his colleagues, night after night, he would be out doing his duty.

She also knew that he was looking forward to retiring from the police service when the war was over and hoped to buy a pub in the country where he could see out his days with a bunch of friendly locals....

She had received the news of his death from her boss Brian Collins. And, as soon as he had asked her to come to his office, the tone of his voice, and the look on his face, let her know that what he was going to say to her would be hard to hear. Her legs found it difficult to keep her up as she followed him down the short corridor; and when he asked her to sit down, she fell into the chair, waiting to hear the worst. He did not draw out her ordeal and told her the essential details with the genuine sympathy that only someone who'd received similar news themselves, knows how to.

When other colleagues got to know, they gave their own versions of sympathy to her; none of which did much to relieve the numbness. One of the technical 'bods' had said to her - that her father. "...Wouldn't have seen, or heard; .....or felt anything, as those new V2 rockets travel at three times the speed of sound. They come from the edge of space; and are completely undetectable; and unfortunately unstoppable." As if that would somehow make her feel better about it.

What compounded her grief was the fact that there was no body, not even any remains. All his warm flesh and blood and all his 'being' ceased to exist in an instant. There was just an unholy blackened crater marking the place where he disappeared from this earth. What sort of world was this where mere men could exert such God-like powers? All she had of him were a few photographs and his meagre possessions - back at her home - to prove to herself that she didn't just dream that he ever existed.

She was shattered: but being at home was not helping her recovery, and she knew she needed to be back at work - to occupy herself with something useful; and there were plenty of useful things that needed doing...

Now all these years later, she hoped that the people in the letters would still be alive.

She knew she had to first find out more about James Edditson. If he was still alive, would it be possible to find him? And if so, what could she possibly say to him?

James had been invalided out of the Navy - after recovering some of his health at 'Haslar' naval hospital in Portsmouth; and returned to his hometown. His replacement on the Hartlepool had emptied his locker and had given the contents to the 'Master at Arms' to be passed onto 'Lighthouse', but they had never made it to him.

Unsurprisingly, the personal effects of junior ratings - even badly injured ones - didn't get a very high priority in wartime. All connection with Marija was lost somewhere between Egypt and England.

The recuperation process had involved re-learning about his previous life and his family. His mother was a great source of strength to him in that regard; as he had tried to be for her.

His father's health though, had continued to deteriorate, and he died a few years after James came home; in 1947. It was a taxing experience for all of them; trying to reconfigure relationships. They were all strangers to him; whilst they all knew him well; or at least the 'old him.' The close bond he once felt towards them could not be as it once was, despite everyone's best endeavours.

The scarring from his burns had healed and faded quite well, his bones had mended, and there was no pain from them anymore; but they were always a constant reminder of what happened to him every time he looked in the mirror. It always felt that there was more missing to his life than just the fact that his memories only began as an injured young man. A restless and unsettled spirit persisted, but the call of adventure was dead.

Kitty had used her previous colleagues' help to trace James; via some unofficial channels and wrote to his last known address on his invalid pension records. She had limited the details of why she needed to contact him after all these years since he had left the navy; merely stating that some information about his time on H.M.S Hartlepool had come to light that she needed to discuss with him. For his part, James had never been keen on knowing any more about a very unpleasant period in his life, as he understood it to be.

After ignoring Kitty's letter to him for a while, the subject came up when talking with his sister Ruby. She understood his reasons for not wanting to 're-live' such difficult times; and offered to meet with Kitty on his behalf just to check out what it was all about. She convinced him he had nothing to lose as she would be very guarded as to what she would disclose to 'the Lady.' He reluctantly agreed; and after some exchanging of correspondence between the two women - later the next month, Kitty was on the train to Oldham, rehearsing in her mind how to explain everything.

They met in Ruby's favourite cafe, and after some initial awkwardness between them; it wasn't long before they were feeling much more comfortable in each other's company. They had a lot to talk about; and after finishing their tea, decided they both could do with a walk. It wasn't far to the local park, and after a couple of hours; long unanswered questions were becoming clearer.

Kitty had brought the letters with her and had intended just to hand them over to Ruby, to pass on to her brother. After their long talk though, she persuaded Ruby that she needed to read them before Kitty returned to London; in case there was anything in them that required further explanation. Ruby knew she had to make James aware of the life and love that had been lost to him; and lost to Marija; and their child: who would now be forty years old.

It would need to be done gently; but too much time had gone by, not to act quickly.

Both women were moved to tears but felt close through their shared sense of sadness at the unfairness of life; as they hugged each other with their goodbyes.

Kitty had told Ruby that she had not made contact with anyone in Malta as it was obviously up to James to decide if that was what he wanted. She had also offered to pay for any of their travel costs if they wanted to go to Malta. There was now no reason or obstacles stopping him from facing his past; except trepidation.

James' recovery had the veneer of success; but underneath the outward signs of normality, the struggle to find the confidence in himself he once had, constantly escaped him. He had become more distant from many of the people he knew before joining the navy.

Even some members of his own family felt quite shut out from him. There were attempts made to rebuild a new life; and he managed to get an office job working for the 'coal board' after the local pit was nationalised. He remained there for some years; where he was content enough, if not fulfilled.   There were many arranged and manoeuvred meetings with potential dates, but nothing had flourished into deeper relationships.

His love of music had never been lost though; and it had got him through the periods in his life when the futility of everything could have overwhelmed him. His biggest achievement was learning to play the piano, and he was now reasonably proficient. He had used his meagre income and savings frugally, and managed to save enough to buy a second hand upright Hoffmann model that dominated the space in the small living room of his rented cottage. It was his most treasured possession. Being able to set his poetry to a piano accompaniment had been the closest he ever came to joy; and purpose. It was music that no one else in the world would ever hear.

He'd also watched his siblings' children - almost from when they came into the world - grow and become independent, contented people. People unlike him; that could relate to an ever changing world without difficulty; and that went on to have children of their own.

While the children were young, he had enjoyed being a part of their journeys: and had always done his best to be the fun uncle that helped them to learn about the world; but it had always been a bitter - sweet experience.

In all of those precious shared moments he spent with them; it brought home to him how much he had missed out on.

When he started reading the first letter, he felt sad: but it was the sadness anyone with any humanity would feel; not the personal reaction he knew he should be feeling. How could he not even remember anything about what must have once been so dear to him? But it was like hearing about someone else's life, not his own. He read on, trying to relate to a reality he couldn't make seem real.

Then Ruby gave him the last letter and stood behind him with her comforting hands on his shoulders. Marija's words were hard to take; but the sight of the small child staring out of the photograph at him; defying the passing of time; crashed into him.

After the initial shock though, he knew why. The thought of opening himself up to past nightmares that he had hitherto, only been informed of; but could not actually remember, was not something he felt well able to deal with, even now. His instincts were to avoid the possible upset that might be caused to all concerned.

Yet he felt obligated to meet them. More than that, he 'wanted' to meet them; not just out of decency and responsibility; but more from a growing sense of needing to make his life have more meaning. For forty years he had trained his mind not to be curious about that part of his life, as it was easier and safer not to. He'd re-learned about his family in Lancashire since his injuries and that was fine. As far as he was concerned, his life began after 1940; and it had been a gradual, safe, improving kind of life; if perhaps, a little devoid of real happiness. This 'secure' life could keep emotion and sentimentality at a safe distance. Now there were feelings flowing through him that he wasn't in control of. Was this a real emotional connection, or just wishful thinking; a compensation for a life lived blandly? How would he know?

The concept of being a father and possibly a grandfather - and what that really entailed was hard to come to terms with. So much to understand; so little time in which to learn. It was taking him to places he'd resigned himself that he would never go to; emotionally, and; if he could be brave enough, literally.

His sister had always been a wise source of inspiration through the years, and since his mother had died, she was his only confidant. Her reliability had been invaluable; now, again; she would be the hand steadying the ship.

Without her, he doubted he would have the resolve or mental resource to deal with the implications of Marija's letters.

It was such a long time ago, though. Like him, she too, must have changed a lot since then. Would she still want to meet him? Would their daughter want to? To complicate things further, even if they did want him back in their lives, there was still the sickening, inescapable fear of letting everyone down by not remembering.

Thank Goodness he had Ruby. She would know just what to say in a letter. Left to his own devices, it would be something he would deliberate on forever and never complete.

Never meant to be.

Marija had named their daughter Silver: it was an unusual choice, but to her, a very obvious one; she would be the embodiment of their shared beam of light. Silver had lived with her strange name for nearly forty years now. She had despised it for half of that time - because of the way it made her feel even more different from the others. But as an adult she learned to enjoy its uniqueness; and it suited her. It had only been through finding her Mother again that its significance was made known to her; and now she cherished it.

After the war; for so many years, Marija had put heart and soul into her struggle to find 'Lighthouse' - but nothing had ever materialised. Every hopeful avenue of inquiry, however promising, always eventually turned out to be a 'cul-de-sac' - just another very dead end. She had kept believing even when any sane person would have given up. Now; only a few years since Silver had been back in Marija's life again; their reconciliation was not proving to be a straightforward process for both parties.

When Silver was first born, she was a wonderful distraction for Marija. She loved Motherhood, and her baby dearly, but during Silver's early years, the lack of news of 'Lighthouse' diminished her ability to care for herself and her child.

Her father's death compounded this; and eventually, Silver needed to be looked after by a cousin, as Marija lost the battle with her grief, later, this role was taken over by the 'Sisters of Dedication.' The convent, taking on the education of Silver, in their own inimitable way. Despite everything, Silver made the most of her time there, showing a natural love of learning, even if the curriculum was somewhat stunted in certain subjects.

After leaving the nuns in the late fifties, her first job was with an estate agency, where the proprietor soon recognised her acumen for business. Luckily for her, although her boss was from a previous and more conservative generation, he was a man with modern ideas. Issac Attard had no children of his own and treated Silver almost like the daughter he never had. He supported her through the years when the discouraging voices and attitudes prevailed, and women who wanted to make their own way in the world were not readily accepted.

By the time she was twenty six, she had her own agency; and two years later, with her partner, had branched into property development. She was doing well, and was living in a beautiful home on the nearby island of Gozzo. Life was very comfortable materially, but there was still that feeling of not really knowing who she was that denied her life its completeness.

The turning point came as she was listening to the radio one afternoon. The song 'Lovechild' was being sung to her; directly to her, by the sweet yet penetrating voice of Diana Ross. The lyrics touched her in a way no other song ever had, and they combined with the sympathetically moving music to magnify the emotional response that flooded over her. It could have been written about her. The way it told her story; growing up feeling all the shame of illegitimacy - she too had been determined not to inflict that on any child of her's.

Now, as a modern woman, she had refused to be defined by the bigotry of outdated attitudes and customs - her life was as legitimate as anyone else's. She had been born with the self- belief to make the most of any opportunity that came her way; despite the discouragement of those who had scorned her for daring to exist. Merely the result of some Godless act of lurid passion. She felt sure her God would want her to flourish, and she wanted to hang on to the dream that the love of two people had created her.

The song sparked in her a new drive to expunge any of the remaining shame and lack of self-worth that had dogged her all of her formative years. Nothing from then on would deter her from finding out about a Mother she only had the faintest of memories of: and a past that had only ever been talked about as being wicked.

Something deep within her had always resisted the indoctrination that would have had her believe that her mother was a sinner and she was a consequence of sin: and so the quest to find Marija began.

Marija had continued to live in her old house, but it was falling further into disrepair as the years went by. It had suffered some damage during the war, and her father had intended to repair it himself; but had only got as far as taking more of it down when he had his heart attack. Since then, it had belonged solely to Marija, but she had little capacity to do much about its further decline. By the sixties, it had gotten so bad that Marija had had to move out and live with a friend, and during this time, her once proud house, continued its sad path towards dereliction. Living away from her home didn't suit Marija, despite the best intentions of her friend.

Fortunately however, Marija received a largesse from the death of a distant relative, and she used the money to get her home repaired well enough for her to return - just a few years before being reunited with Silver.

By the time Silver had 'found' her Mother again though, neither Marija or her house were doing that well. Silver could easily get her company to rebuild the house properly - and relatively quickly, but her mother would take more time. Silver's first meeting with Marija was as shocking as she had feared.

Marija looked hollowed out, almost as if her loss of all that was dear to her, left her just the shell of what she used to be. Her face sunken and sallow, her frame frail, and skinny.

Silver had no memory of living where she had been born. She'd been taken away from it - to be looked after by others - when she was barely three. But the house was easy to find. Its address was the only useful piece of information that the convent had retained about her past; and with her negotiation skills - it hadn't been difficult to obtain....

That first day she drove along the road admiring the glimpses of the attractive harbour - conscious that she was likely to be retracing the journeys her mother used to take in the carefree times of her youth. She knew at once when she had reached her destination; her birth place.

Slowly entering through its open gateway, she found a shady place to park her car. Retrieving her handbag from the front passenger seat, she got out and leaned against its side to 'take in' the atmosphere of her surroundings. A mixture of impressions came to her as the place welcomed her - in the same intangible way it must have warmed the hearts of generations before her.

Despite its outward 'tired' appearance, much of the structure of the house was still quite sound - retaining a proud, and almost cheerfully resilient dignity. And, she imagined; if its old stones could speak - they could tell of joyful times 'aplenty.'

Looking up at the upper floor though, she noticed the poor workmanship of the recent repairs, and allowed herself a wry smile. They were definitely not carried out to a standard that she approved of. She realised, even on that first viewing - that sections of it would have to be taken down again, in order to effect a renovation that would do justice to the home's proud heritage.

After their emotionally draining first meeting with each other, Silver brought Marija to a restaurant to give her a good meal but she was just picking at her food. The music in the background was pleasant enough but easily ignored until a particular song demanded her attention. 'Broken-down angel' by a band (who she found out later were called 'Nazareth') was now strangely telling Marija's story. Coincidence? Or was she just looking for connections and reasons? Was Marija 'only a broken-down angel'? 'A child that lost her way'...? Silver convinced herself that was exactly what she was seeing in front of her....

Marija had never left her island all her life; nor had she moved out of the shadow of the person she used to be, during that special time. For her, every day was lived in 1940.

The arrival of the letter from 'lighthouse' was a 'bolt from the blue:' and so very hard to deal with. It had been delivered, looking inconspicuous enough.

Josie picked it up - along with the rest of the mail that day, and put them all in the drawer of the 'hall-stand.' Josie had been employed by Silver, to be Marija's 'live-in' carer, in the hope that this would only be a temporary position, until Marija had finished her convalescence. It would mean that Marija would be able to stay living in her old house. And; apart from disappointment; it was practically the only constant in her life - that was warm and familiar to her.

It soon became clear though, that Josie would probably be needed indefinitely. She had become adept at giving just the right amount of help required, to lessen the stresses and responsibilities of modern life - while still allowing Marija her feeling of independence.

She gave the letters to Silver, as she always did when she visited, so that Silver could deal with them without Marija having to worry about them. They had the outward appearance of a regular mix of welcome, and not so welcome demands on her time; and Josie made no mention that there was anything out of the ordinary amongst them.

Later that evening when Silver was at her home, she went through them - to see if there was anything that needed to be acted upon by her.

Almost at once, the white envelope with an English stamp and postmark caught her attention; but the way Marija's name was written, really 'jumped out' at her. The 'M' was noticeably larger than the rest of her first name, which in turn was larger than her surname. Each letter was clear and unmistakable, despite its cursive style. It was unusual; yet she knew she'd seen it before. It took a few seconds for her to make the connection.

Marija had kept all of the letters that 'Lighthouse' had sent to her, before he disappeared from her life - each one in its original envelope. Silver had read them all, in secret, after going through her mother's things; and it had convinced her even more, that she must have been conceived from love. And yet tragically, ironically, she almost wished she hadn't been. It would have surely been all so much easier for her mother to bear, if she had had no deep feelings for the 'person;' Silver now strongly suspected, was her father.

When she had read - in the last letter to Marija; of how wonderful 'this person' had felt in her mother's arms; and the other beautifully quaint way he expressed his love for her; it was 'sweet.' But it was made all the more bitter and sinister, to know that nothing more was ever written by him again. Just years of deafening silence….

It affected Silver in all sorts of ways that she hadn't fully anticipated.

She had felt uncomfortable, and conflicted at first, as to whether it was right to intrude into the private thoughts, wishes and promises made by her Mother's lover, but had concluded that reading his side of things was absolutely necessary.

But learning of the overwhelming feelings they had for each other; caused her to shed many tears - something she rarely allowed herself to do - and she had needed a lot of support from her own partner to come to terms with it all.

Now; this new pristine envelope, looking so similar to those treasured ones - from so long ago - flashed in front of her eyes, almost as if it was trying to make her believe that the last forty years, never really existed.

Silver felt herself shiver as her pulse quickened. She looked hard at the postmark. It was definitely from England: and Marija never received letters from England. Part of her wanted to tear it open; but she controlled that impulse and sat with it in her hands while conflicting emotions vied to be acted on. After a couple minutes, she found herself carefully taking the contents from the envelope, but it was like she was watching someone else do it.

Unfolding it, her eyes immediately went to the address at the top right. 'Oldham, Lancashire.'

The old letters were always written from H.M.S. Hartlepool; but in one of them, Silver distinctly remembered that Marija's lover had mentioned that he came from a place called Oldham in Lancashire, and that one day - he would take her there….

Silver read on.

'Dear Marija,

I hope this letter finds you well. My name is James Eddiston, but you may also have known me by my nickname of 'Lighthouse.' I have only recently been informed that we once knew each other well and that we had a child together, some time in 1940. For my part, unfortunately, I knew nothing of this, due to an injury I received at that time whilst serving on board my ship. I have suffered from amnesia ever since and…..'

She had to stop reading, and actively try to focus on staying calm. But it was futile. How could fate have been so cruel to us? She screamed inside. Anger; joy; frustration; sorrow; were causing her emotions to rage through her, making it difficult to think straight. She wanted to go to her mother immediately, and 'yell' the wonderful news to her, but somehow her rational self won out, and restrained her. That clearly would not be sensible. Her own head was in enough of a 'whirl', how could she make such shocking news manageable, to such a fragile old lady.

She had to get herself 'together' before she could possibly be of any help. Delivering such potentially disturbing news needed a lot more skill than she possessed at that moment. It was all too outrageously unbelievable, even for her to accept.

After some days of talking things through with her partner and friends, she drew up a plan of how she would let her mother know.

Despite the careful way she told her mother, Marija was left dazed and numb by the news. Too much emotion had already racked her weary mind to be able to deal with this; she said nothing; but eventually, she reacted with just very gentle sobbing. Her tears, trickling their way down a face that had grown used to them, over the many sad years - and which Silver could not quell.

Even with all of Silver's comforting words, and reassuring embraces - she was inconsolable...

But new days dawn; and Silver was only too aware that there may not be that many days left for her 'parents' - that word 'parents;' still tricky for her to get used to. She also knew she must be the one to write back to 'Lighthouse:' her 'father;' her actual, real father...

The reply was incredibly hard to get right though and she'd screwed up many failed attempts, before she produced a version that felt good enough.

She decided she would write it as if it had been written by Marija herself; and on balance, thought it expedient, not to give a lot of detail as to what had happened in the intervening years, as it might do more harm than good. And anyway; it was impossible to convey even a fraction of what she wanted to say. She had to be content knowing that:- 'almenu ghamit bidu' - 'at least she had made a start.' And a letter was now on its way to England.

Meanwhile, its recipient was trying to learn anew about Malta, hoping something would jog his reluctant memory. He had stared for hours at the photo of Marija - with its Maltese background, wanting to believe he recognised something. But he was fighting a broken mind to get back there; and fearing that he may break the rest of himself in the process.

Lancashire England 1997.
Reflection.

"That was a lovely tribute the vicar gave for Ruby wasn't it Jack?" "So true about people leaving their mark on the world in different ways - some in monuments of stone or steel; others with words or ideas; and some like her, who leave their's, through the kindness they give to every one that knows them." As the man was speaking, Jack thought he recognised something about the voice. He looked at the man's receding grey hair and slightly moist eyes.

They were smiling a somewhat familiar warmth towards him, despite the sadness of the occasion. Jack continued to look at him for a second - as he tried to find the appropriate response, "Yes, it was very fitting, I thought." "Lovely words for a lovely Lady." Jack, too, had found the whole service unexpectedly very moving, and when at the end, they played the colliery brass band tunes that had been such an influence on her early life, he hadn't been able to stop himself from welling up. His feelings were also tempered with guilt, though. He remembered his early years going to see his Grandmother and somewhat took for granted the warmness of her personality, whenever she greeted him. Shamefully, in recent years, he'd hardly seen her. In fact, when he really thought about it, he hadn't seen her since he'd got married.

"So what are you doing with yourself these days Jack?" "Are you still with the Fire Service?"

. "Yer 'fraid so; been there for nearly twenty years now; looking forward to retirement in a couple of years." "Oh, okay, what are you planning to do then?" That question stumped him; he didn't really know, and after struggling to come up with something amusing to say, just resorted to an obvious and boring reply about relaxing more and travelling.

David's next comments tested his conversational skills further. David was the eldest son of Ruby and James' younger brother Ralph, and although he just about worked out who he was talking to, Jack realised he'd never actually spoken to him before as an adult. He knew almost nothing about him and although David seemed to know the basics about him, it brought home the fact that his parents' move down South had isolated them from their roots in the mining community they had all once lived in.

They continued talking, catching up on the many years since they last met; while the rest of the room were in more familiar conversations with each other: and Jack had mentioned what he first did after leaving school at sixteen. "That sounds a bit like my uncle James." David informed him. "He spent some time in the navy during the war." "He got invalided out, I think and then became a bit of a recluse." "Don't remember seeing him much since I was a kid."

After a little awkward silence shared between the two men - each having their own regretful thoughts adding to the solemnity of the day; David came back to their conversation first; with a tried and tested 'filler' and asked. "What made you join the 'fire service' when you left the navy then, Jack?"

The question jerked Jack's thoughts back to the room and then, in order to answer his question, to his early days in the navy when he went to H.M.S. Pheonix, the navy's fire training base.

There, they had very effective ways of imparting vital knowledge about the awesome ways and wants of fire. One of these involved gathering their trainees around a very large tray of oil, which, once lit from one end by an instructor, quickly; but un-remarkably, spread a low flame over its entire surface. To Jack and the others gathered around, the warmth it provided was welcome, but in and of itself, it held little interest to them: as did the instructor's commentary about the things they should know about oil fires.

After a few minutes of the lecture though, he told them all to step a few more paces back while he went to the base of a tower. Up until then, they hadn't taken much notice of its lattice steel framework that rose about twenty feet above one side of the tray; nor the unremarkable piece of rope hanging down from it. The 'talk' that had been delivered to them, flatly and with a distinct lack of passion - by a man who had quite obviously given it many times before - was about to conclude. Without ceremony, he announced to his unimpressed audience. "And this is what happens when you fight an oil fire with water."

He then tugged the rope, which then tipped a bucket over, revealing its hidden contents.

Ordinary, plain, and simple water began its acceleration under the natural influence of gravity. The onlookers had no time to think through any significance of the innocuous looking spectacle, before the water smashed into the burning oil. Instantly, much of the tray's contents vaporised, forming a huge fireball. For a split second, it consumed the air in front of them; literally taking their breath away as it roared up, as if released from a different world none of them had ever known. The desired effect was achieved; being so close to such an elemental force of nature, left no one in doubt as to the point of the lecture. All nonchalance would be forever chastened...

Back in the room, Jack's own cascade of recall went on to reflect on his first real act of fire fighting.

It began with the ship's 'Tannoy' system announcing starkly: "Fire; fire; fire; fire in the gear room." Standing sea fire-fighting party close up." " This is not an exercise"...

After a long spell of watch-keeping, he'd been given the opportunity to be on 'day work,' but this had strings attached, 'day work' consisted mainly of maintenance tasks, and it had been a pleasant change to be able to sleep at night like a normal human being; but there was an additional role to having that perk.

Day workers in the engineering branch, were the ship's 'fire brigade.' If a fire broke out anywhere, that could not be extinguished by personnel 'on-scene,' the buck stopped with them. As one of the old chiefs had relayed to him once: "You can't dial 999 when you're a couple of thousand miles from shore, son"...

He'd only been doing the job for a month or so; and had completed a few refresher training sessions on how to use the aqueous foam forming equipment, better known as 'A triple F.' - as he was now one of the two 'fear-nought suit men.' They would be needed only if there was a major fire on the ship, as minor fires were dealt with by the 'first aid' fire team who would 'attendo-pronto' - using the appropriate hand held extinguishers (CO_2, foam, or water types). It was thought highly unlikely that he and 'Dusty' Miller (The other 'fear-nought suit man) would ever be needed in earnest, for a real major fire, but he knew the drill, he needed to leave what he was doing and 'muster' with the rest of the fire party.

As he arrived at the muster point, the petty officer coordinating, had also just arrived and was being briefed by the 'stoker' who had first spotted the fire while on his 'rounds.' The gear room had two huge gearboxes housed in it, each of which had to integrate the driveshafts of two of the steam turbines and two of the gas turbines.

Most of the time (and for the sake of economy), each gearbox would only be transferring the power of the steam turbines, but when maximum speed was required, the gas turbines would be 'flashed up' and would then add their contribution to the tens of thousands of shaft horsepower being sent through them.

The gear room also housed tanks containing hundreds of gallons of lubricating and hydraulic oil; and it seemed that the fire was situated close by to them.

The 'first aid' fire team were quickly dispatched with the hope they could contain the fire, while he and Dusty were being helped by other members of the fire party to get into their suits and put on their breathing apparatus. He remembered the unexpected sense of calmness he felt as the checks were being done and the time remaining for his air supply was recorded on the white board. The rest of the fire party were connecting canvas fire hoses to the ship's fire main - operating at a pressure of one hundred and twenty pounds per square inch. They also brought the 5 gallon drums of A.F.F. that, once stabbed with an FB5X Venturi pipe - would be instantly connected to a fire hose, ready for the contents to be sucked out and into the hose's seawater, the instant the nozzle was opened. The resultant mixing with the seawater, producing copious gallons of foam ready to be spewed out to form a suffocating blanket for the fire.

As the face mask went on, the hiss from the non-return valve informed him how fast he was breathing - yet the calmness remained within him, and a kind of resignation he'd never experienced before kept him focused on what needed to be done. He went over the procedure in his mind. Dusty would have one hose that would be set to 'water-wall,' providing a fine spray that would shield both of them from much of the heat from the fire, while he would shoot through that wall with the foam on the base of the fire. Having visited the gear room many times though, in his watch-keeping days, he knew if they had to enter the room rather than fight the fire from above in the corridor; it would be difficult, with all their gear, to get through the hatch and down its ladder.

Communicating with each other once their face masks were on, was limited to muffled shouts and visual signals. Communication with the rest of the fire party, once they moved off down the corridor, would be non-existent.

The first aid firefighters had returned saying that they had managed to discharge the contents of a couple of extinguishers in the general direction of the fire but had been forced back as the smoke was starting to choke them. They hadn't managed to put it out. It was up to them now.

A member of the fire party released the clips and opened the steel door leading to the last section of corridor before the gear room and it was immediately apparent why the first aid team had had to retreat. They could just make out the (still open) gear room hatch which was billowing thick black smoke towards them. The impunity the breathing apparatus gave them - from what would otherwise, suffocate them within minutes - enabled them to continue; but It looked bad.

They heaved their 'charged' hoses and the rest of their gear towards the hatch. The exhalation 'hiss' was now much louder in his ears and repeating so much faster - not all attributable to the recent exertion. Hearing his own breath almost to the exclusion of anything else resounded in his head, and he had to concentrate on ignoring it. He knew dwelling on the thought that he may be hearing his last few, would be, to say the least, unhelpful!

The smoke was making visibility difficult, but they had trained how to make their way in conditions like that. Every movement had to be thought through but with, at best, only muffled communication between them, working in tandem was tricky.

Arriving at the hatch moments later, there was no expected orange glow. Nor was there any sensation of heat that despite wearing the thick fear-nought suit, you would still feel when you were close to a big fire.

The electrical lighting was operating, and by looking down through the hatch, it was possible to make out some of the gear room through the smoke, apart from what appeared to be its source. The sense of relief was joyous: and it didn't take long to dispel the adage of, 'there's no smoke without fire.' There definitely was plenty of smoke: but whatever fire there may have been was no longer there. The 'first on scene' guys must have done a better job than they had realised.

His mind then raced on to another fire-fighting connection to his time in the navy. A year or so later, in his last year before leaving the service, he'd been sent up to the outskirts of Birmingham. There, he'd been called upon to be in charge of one of the 'Green Goddess' - the old ex-army fire engines used during the fireman's strike in late 1977. And although recalling his time there would give him some quirky anecdotes that he could talk about ; they didn't really explain the real reason.

These memories compressed into a few seconds of pause - reminding him why life had unwound as it had, but it hadn't given him anything that was succinct and witty enough to progress the conversation with the man in front of him waiting for a reply, and he had to resort to another bland response.

"Didn't really have any other better options I suppose; and it was something I already knew something about."

Island Reunion. Malta 1980 (validation)

James Eddiston stared again at the photo of his baby daughter and compared it to the photo she had sent in reply to his recent letter. A beautiful woman who had grown up and had children of her own; all while he was still living in oblivion. He wiped his eyes to stop his tears from damaging the precious images of a lost parenthood that never was and put the precious images back in the wallet. The plane would be landing in five minutes, and the announcement had been made to 'fasten his seat belt.' He'd gone over so many times, ways he could greet two people that were so special to him in their different ways; but that were both complete strangers. None of them seemed anything like adequate for the situation.

In the end, though, it was taken out of his hands. Silver came up to him, and embraced him. She had picked him out easily from the other tourists filing through the airport. He was clearly a lost and bewildered man caught in the blinding searchlight of change; somewhat frail and tentative; and trying to deal with fast-moving upheaval.

The emotional closeness between them was immediate; but he was too choked to say anything and just drank in her affection.

Silver drove him to Rinella bay and as he got out of her car he could see her sitting on a bench silhouetted against the sun. Silver walked him over to her Mother, and said "There is someone here we've waited a long time to meet." Marija got to her feet, and as James approached her, she reached out both her hands for his. Then they stood there, with so much needing to be said; but both unable to find words; as they looked out at their Mediterranean. A Theatre of blue that had brought them together and swept them apart.

Time had taken their youth from them, yet the old beach front where they once shared their love for each other; had a mask of newness hiding its once natural and familiar appeal. It now embraced the appearance of the modern world. A world neither of them had ever properly managed to come to terms with. Her face was wrinkled, but her eyes and the expression they projected had not really changed. He looked down at her hands; again now aged; but as he reached out to hold them, their touch still retained a softness that belied their appearance. There was some attraction there but no real recollection; it was just too long ago. He knew he should be feeling more than awkwardness, but this first meeting was disturbing rather than stirring. He begged his mind to give him some recognition of their time together; but nothing came.

Marija looked at, and into the old man that stood before her. Despite the preparation Silver had given, she too, needed to adjust. The projection of the man she had envisaged was not what was confronting her now. His thinning white hair was a little longer than she had known it, and there were many lines and creases on his face that had not been there before, but his smile was the same. The way it combined with his eyes and the rest of his face had not altered. When she looked more closely, she could see the scarring; but it was not as obvious as Silver had warned it might be. In fact, the ravages of time alone - on a face last seen in the pristine glow of youth, was harder to adjust to.

Their daughter looked at them, and saw their struggle. She knew that this was never going to be easy. The people they were then, no longer existed. Lost decades could never be re-found; but just maybe, lost loves could be re-grown, from the dust of now. Was there any seed; that, like the poppy, could still be waiting for their ground to be disturbed?

Leaving them standing together, much more as strangers than lovers; she walked back to the car to get a cassette player. She hoped that by playing them their song, it would help in the re-capturing of what they'd experienced so long ago. Now was the moment to play it.

The first few bars of the beautiful orchestration rang out clear and authentic, before starting to muffle; and, in another second, distort horribly. Frantically she stopped the machine and opened the front drawer. A thin brown strip of magnetic tape had spilled out from the safe and secure confines of the cassette spools, and had become entrapped within the other workings of the machine. There was a moment where they all did or said nothing; before Silver composed herself and thought about what to do next.There was nothing for it other than gingerly pulling and teasing out the chaos of screwed up loops. A couple of feet of twisted and creased tape - that should so cleverly be capable of reproducing their sweet music; dangled out forlornly as her parents looked on.

Silver spoke calmly to them, disguising her true fear. Her hopes and dreams for them seemed to be hanging beyond her grasp.

Carefully, she started untwisting and smoothing the precious brown ribbon between her fingers. Then, taking a pencil from her hand bag, she used it to slowly wind a section at a time, of the more organised and straightened tape, back onto the machine's reels. After several minutes of intense concentration, the mess started to look more orderly: and the last disorganised tangle was back in place.

This time when Silver pressed 'play;' the youthful voice of Irving Berlin managed to sing to them; albeit with a little warbling in places;

but it rang out nevertheless; strident and 'un-aged.' It blended with the music as wonderfully as ever, and its melodies swept over them and into them, touching parts of deep subconsciousness.

Marija had herself brought something for their reunion. James had always challenged the blind faith she had in her religion; and he debated with her about it many times. There were also the many irrational superstitions she held. He had believed that nothing should be taken for granted and be beyond questioning; but she had found it all too radical and disturbing to contemplate. This inspired him to write a song for her.

She had brought the lyrics with her and took them from the pocket of her dress, and handed them to him. James looked at the words he had written to her and slowly read them through, more than once. The style of the handwriting was familiar, and to a lesser extent, so was the paper it was written on, although now 'yellowed' with age. He had to ask himself though; who was this young man - so sure he had all the answers? Now the reader, forty years older, was confident of so very little anymore. But gradually, the time-worn piece of paper was beginning to reacquaint James with the writer and the thoughts behind the words written on it. They began to spring some meaning, after at first seeming quite bizarre and difficult to relate to. Now; trickling on from them, came feelings that ran clearer, and were flowing back to a past that had laid dry and dormant for so long....

But there is us …. A song for Marija

There may only be the air of yesterday

Inside a crystal ball - No portal to the supernatural

Just confidence tricks at play…

And whatever's seen in the tarot cards

Is just what you want them to say.

But there is us, to place your trust in

It's only your love, that I must win

Of all the world, to take great care in

A providence I, can always share in

There may be no such thing as destiny

To control a chaotic world -

Nothing preordained to be unfurled

Just the certainty of mortality

And blankets of comfort to be found

That warm the coldness of reality.

But there is us to place our faith in

Its only with you, this world has grace in

Not all things can be known for certain

Somethings will remain beyond that curtain

70

But there is a love that never grows cold

An ever-present hand to hold

And however our adventure unfolds

It will be our story that is told

"You know you gave me the words to your song, and I've thought about them a lot over the years; but you never sang me the tune." Lighthouse stared at her. He knew they'd been 'sleeping' through their spring, summer, and probably most of their autumn; but the sun was shining on them today. A reviving friendly sun, that was ending the time of hibernation. He smiled at her for a long time, before whispering. "Well, if truth be told, I don't know if I ever had a proper tune to them." "...But with your help, I think we can come up with one now...."

2022: tislima ghall-imhabba
(a salute to love)

"What about Malta?" Hannah said, handing him the holiday brochure. Its cover showed a view of Valletta and Grand harbour by night. "Wow," he said; "I haven't seen that sight for well over forty years." "Yer, I thought you told me you'd been there when you were in the navy." "It'll be great to have a proper holiday - now that things are starting to be more normal again."

Hannah had been married to Jack Thompson for all of that forty years as well. They had met in Portsmouth while Jack was still in the navy and had married a few years later. Jack had left the navy in 1978 and had worked for the fire service since then; only recently retiring. He started his civilian career driving a fire engine, but for the last ten years he'd only been driving a desk. Their three children had long since grown up and left home, and they hadn't had a foreign holiday for quite a few years.

"Okay," he said "I'd love to see some of the old sites again - It looks a good deal; why don't you book it up? I'll show you where I spent some of my miss-spent youth."

The flight to Malta international airport didn't take long, and on the descent, towards the islands, they were struck by just how small they looked. Even the larger main island of Malta; less than seventeen miles long and nine miles wide, seemed 'lost' against the great sea that wrapped around them.

They collected the hire car and headed for their hotel. For the first few days, they visited the beaches on the main Island and took the ferry to the smaller and more rural island of Gozo. They explored some fascinating historic sites, such as the ruined megalithic temples that were older than Stonehenge or the Egyptian pyramids; and went for a fantastic snorkel at the blue grotto. Next on their itinerary, they thought they'd explore Valletta, and Jack was looking forward to showing Hannah some of the places he'd known before they'd met. He was also keen to visit the National War Museum at Fort St. Elmo, where he'd read that one of the original Gloucester Sea Gladiators was housed.

At the museum, they were quite shocked to learn that when Malta entered the war, there had been just three Sea Gladiator biplanes to defend the island; even back in 1940, they were pretty old, slow, and out of date.The three aircraft were named 'Faith,' 'Hope,' and 'Charity;' and it was 'Faith' that had survived; and was in front of them to tell its valiant story. Despite not being at the cutting edge of enemy aircraft interception, these gladiators of the air had given quite a good account of themselves against waves of Italian bombers flying from nearby Sicily, trying to terrify the civilian population into submission. As the bombing got worse on Malta, Hawker Hurricanes were later brought in by aircraft carriers to reinforce the Island's air defences. But it had been the three old 'string-bags' that had been the original stalwarts.

Churchill had called Malta itself an "unsinkable aircraft carrier," and he'd been very keen that it didn't fall into enemy hands due to its strategic proximity to North Africa. As the 'Axis' campaign escalated, though; many more Italian bombers - joined by German Stukas also based in Sicily - had done their best to 'sink' the islands. As a result, little Malta achieved the unenviable record of having endured the most sustained period of bombing - 154 consecutive days and nights from April 1942; than anywhere else on earth!

The 'Siege' had become so bad that the island was almost starved into capitulation, before; finally, a battered convoy of ships eventually made it into the harbour with some supplies, on August 15th.

After the war, in tribute to their prolonged ordeal, all the people of Malta were awarded the George Cross, the highest civilian medal of bravery. Although proud of the recognition they received from Britain; many Maltese would have preferred some more material investment in their reconstruction: and the notion of independence from Britain was growing.

Jack and Hannah were just about to leave Valletta when he realised that he hadn't yet shown her Custom House Steps, where the small boats called dghajsas used to ferry ship's crews to and from their ships. It was at this point that he remembered the night he'd missed the last one back to his ship, and as he recalled he shared the story with her. She said, "Well, it's still quite early; why don't we have a walk around the harbour together?"

The walk was very different to how he remembered it. A lot more building had taken place, during all those years he'd been away, and he couldn't be sure of the route he took, as, looking back, it all seemed a little vague. There were so many more streets and houses than he remembered, and there was a whole new part of the harbour side that had been constructed to allow much bigger ships to dock there; it looked so different to him. Malta had gained independence from Britain in 1964, but it wasn't until March 31st, 1979 when all British forces left the islands; that the people felt fully independent enough to celebrate that day as 'Freedom Day.' Since then, the towns had modernised tremendously.

Eventually, they found themselves in a less built up part of the harbour, and it was starting to look a little more familiar. Its rugged ancient charm was just as he had remembered. The sky; starting to turn various hues of pink and orange, was now contrasting beautifully with the vast blue of the Mediterranean. The same, enduring Mediterranean that had been the life-blood of the island from prehistoric times and through all the machinations, invention, and life and death struggles of many great civilisations since. It was easy to look beyond some of the reminders of modern Malta and sense its timeless appeal. It felt magical.

They walked together and continued to soak up the historic atmosphere until he caught sight of a solid looking building. Getting closer to it; it struck him that something about it seemed strange. It wasn't just that it appeared to have been built fairly recently and yet was constructed mainly of old blocks of stones - there were other buildings like that; it was just its situation; and how it seemed to fit and 'live' in the landscape.

As they approached the front of the building, he was intrigued to see an intricately carved door with four stained glass windows depicting various maritime scenes. What astounded him though, was what surrounded the door. Its elaborate frame immediately revived hazy images of the place, in a previous time. That very strange Maltese night nearly half a century ago. He'd never seen a building anything like it before or since; it had to be the same one.

He stood there admiring its charm and trying to reminisce about that night; when; the door opened Interrupting his deep train of thought, a young woman came out. The day's waning light, rich and rosy, reflected from her, and seemed to give her an almost ethereal appearance. She had the same dark eyes and raven hair as the girl from all those years ago. Instantly connecting him to a time long since past. A time when the original old building remained in its place but was wounded; and, like a desperate and confused dog, had bitten him. He relived the falling; then the vivid splendour of the place and the enchantment of that young woman that now seemed to confront him again. Her name came back to him, and impulsively he blurted out "Marija?" ....

"What?" "No." The young woman replied, with a mixture of amusement and some concern in the tone of her voice.

"My name is Emalie." "Marija was my Great Grandmother's name, though - she used to live here." "Did you know her?"

Recollections from when he was a young man collided and conflicted with the more rational reasoning of a more worldly wise one, but it was difficult to reconcile the two. He stared at her in stunned silence for some time.

Seeing Jack's confusion, Hannah felt she needed to help explain things to an increasingly bewildered young woman. " Hello, Emalie; we're on holiday, this is my husband, Jack, and I'm Hannah." "It's just that Jack remembers being here a long time ago… when he was in the navy: and he was just showing me the sights." After another awkward silence ensued, during which Emalie continued trying to weigh up, just who they might possibly be; and why they would be there, she asked them. "What sights? You're quite some way from any of the usual sights here." "Yes; we are;" Hannah quickly replied, "but we're retracing a memorable walk around the harbour Jack made."

"I see." except she didn't: and Hannah didn't feel Emalie would have the time or interest to want to listen to any more of a detailed explanation. Instead she asked about what she assumed was the name plaque for the house; next to the still slightly open, front door.

It was made from a dark maroon/brown wood; about two feet wide, and a foot high, but - irregular in shape, and at least three inches thick. Hannah guessed it must have once been part of an old boat. Written on it, in black letters surrounded by a white shadow border, were the words:- 'dar tal-holm tieghi.' Pointing at it, Hannah asked, "Is that the Maltese name of this lovely house Emilie?" "Yes," she answered. .."And does the 'holm' part mean 'home' in English?" "No," she corrected, "actually 'holm' or 'holma' means 'dream, and 'dar' means home. As far as I know, it is what this house has always been called…. Marija's grandfather must have been very proud of what he had built here, to call it: 'home of my dreams,' I guess."

"Ah that's beautiful", Hannah smiled back. Then, dismissing her initial thoughts of being impertinent, said. "If you don't mind me asking, what does that other plaque say?" Emalie was equivocal, should she tell them? Was there a genuine connection between the man and a Great Grandmother she'd never met and knew little about? Or was it prudent to give little information away to strangers?

In the end her curiosity won out and she said to Hannah. "My Grandmother - Marija's daughter, had the house rebuilt some time in the late seventies I think." "It had become quite derelict after the war; but as I said, it has belonged in our family for many years before that."

"I have asked my mother about it, but all she really knew was that it was written by Marija; and, her daughter Silver, my grandmother, had the plaque made.." "I have read it many times and wondered about it; but a few years ago I did my best to translate it into English for part of a literacy assignment I was working on." "Some of it is difficult to translate directly; but I'll show you what I've written, and you can tell me if it has any relevance to you."

She disappeared inside the house but quickly returned and handed them a piece of paper.

Hannah read it slowly out loud.

To the rest of the world, you never existed,

But for that precious time (we shared)

You existed more than the rest of the world.

Those fleeting moments you were mine

In all your magnificence and presence

I thrived in the warmth and light from your soul.

Then, then, all those years of darkness

Yet wilting in the heat of the sun

The two of us lost at sea

While the slow endurance of unfeeling time,

Demanded repayment on the loan of joy it had allowed us.

Until that day the debt was paid; and you came back to me

Damaged and broken, your warmth and light faded

But once more again, we danced

By the glimmer of our flickering flame

And remembered together what love was

Before all trace of our shadows cast no more on our sweet land.

Emalie was the first to speak. "Well, Jack, you've heard what Marija had to say, so did you know her?"

Jack was still staring at the young woman in front of him, and it was difficult to find his voice; but after what seemed an uncomfortable amount of time to all of them, he answered. "I don't know…"

Milton Keynes UK
Ingram Content Group UK Ltd.
UKHW051354110224
437549UK00007B/75

9 781915 904522